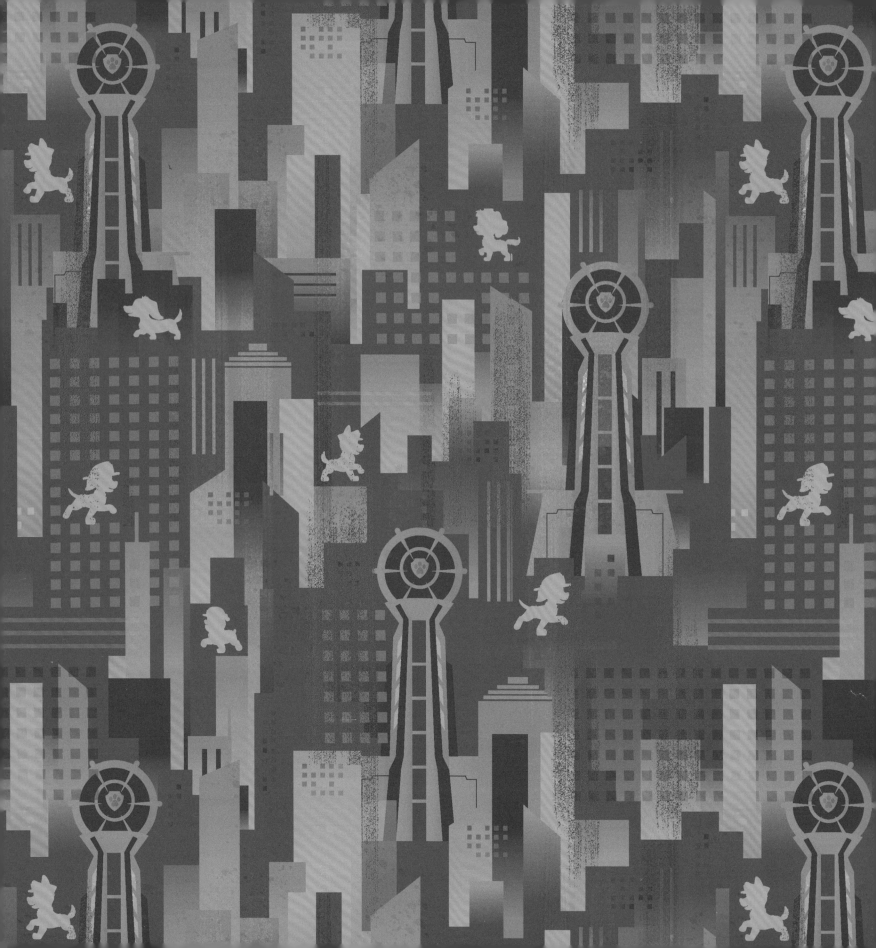

This PAW Patrol story book belongs to

Staś

Farshore

First published in the United States 2021 by Penguin Random House
This edition published in Great Britain 2021 by Farshore

An imprint of HarperCollins*Publishers*
1 London Bridge Street, London SE1 9GF
www.farshore.co.uk

HarperCollins*Publishers*
1st Floor, Watermarque Building, Ringsend Road
Dublin 4, Ireland

Written by Nicole Johnson
Based on the screenplay by Billy Frolick and Cal Bunker & Bob Barlen
Based on the story by Billy Frolick
Illustrated by Wedoo Studio

ISBN 978 0 7555 0291 2
Printed in the UK
002

A CIP catalogue record for this title is available from the British Library.

FSC
www.fsc.org

MIX
Paper from
responsible sources
FSC® C007454

BIG CITY ADVENTURES

In bustling Adventure City, there lived a little pup named Liberty. She knew all her neighbours and everything that went on around town.

"Tony!" she said one day, greeting a friend while out for a walk. "How's the fruit business?"

"It would be better if I wasn't always giving you free fruit," he joked while giving her some strawberries.

Liberty thanked him and continued on her walk.

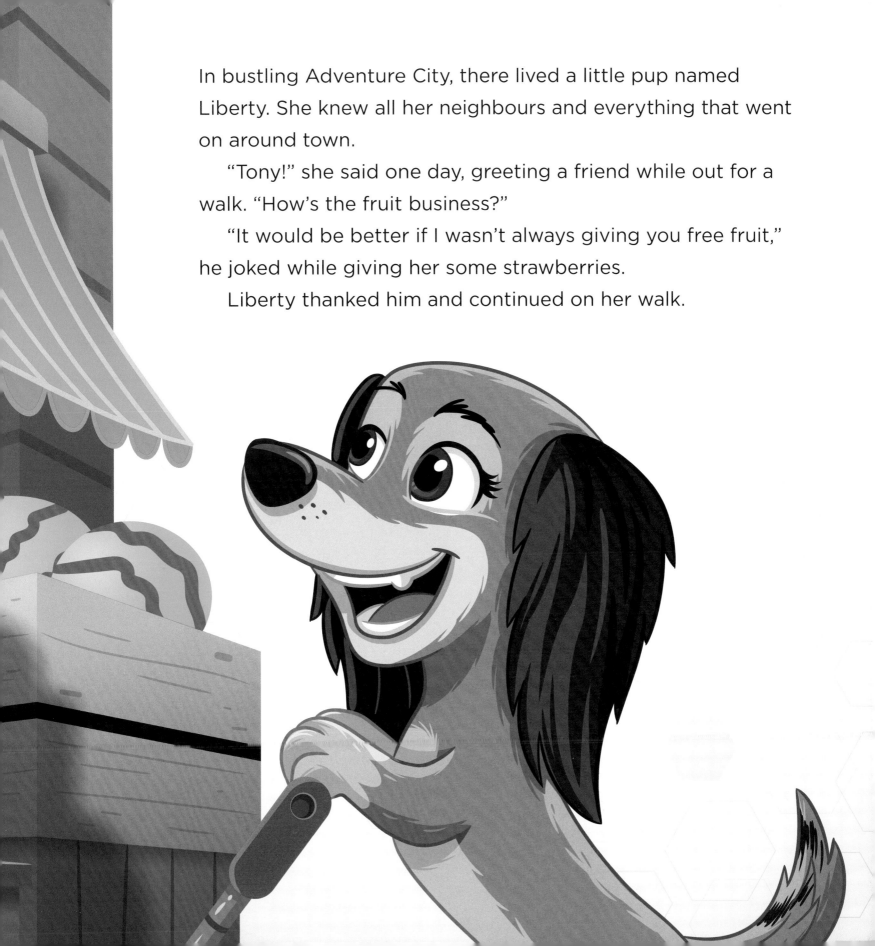

Liberty loved her home and worked hard to keep it clean and safe — just like her heroes, the PAW Patrol!

When she stepped onto the train, she saw a man littering.

"Hey!" she said. "You pick that up and put it in the bin."

After the man had cleaned up his rubbish, Liberty thanked him.

"We've gotta take pride in our city!" she said.

Liberty left the train station and came upon a big, busy event. It was the inauguration of Adventure City's new mayor — the awful Mayor Humdinger!

Liberty knew just what to do — call the PAW Patrol!

Humdinger had been the mayor of Foggy Bottom and almost destroyed the town, so Ryder knew the people of Adventure City needed help.

Ryder told Liberty they would be there right away.

Later that day, Mayor Humdinger was at his first event as mayor — an Adventure City fireworks show. Mayor Humdinger wanted big fireworks, so he pressed all the buttons at once! Fireworks and rockets exploded in all directions, causing huge fires everywhere!

Liberty rushed to get help and found Ryder and the pups stuck in traffic! She jumped into Ryder's car.

"I'm Liberty," she said. "I know this city like the back of my paw. I'll get you where you need to be!"

As fireworks exploded everywhere, Liberty showed the team a shortcut to city hall.

At city hall, Liberty watched the PAW Patrol launch into action.
Marshall put out the fireworks, and Rocky scooped them up.
Ryder and the pups had saved the day!

After the rescue, people swarmed the PAW Patrol to take pictures and say thanks.

"Anyone want a picture with me?" Liberty asked the crowd of fans. "I'm kind of like an honorary member of the PAW Patrol!" No one was interested in Liberty. But her chance to help would come soon!

The next day, Liberty watched the PAW Patrol complete another amazing rescue. But then Ryder and Chase got into a disagreement, and Chase ran away. Ryder ran after him. When he turned a corner, all he found was Chase's tracking collar. Chase was gone!

Luckily, street-smart Liberty knew everyone on that block! She asked all the shop owners if they had seen Chase.

At a small corner shop, the group learned that many dogs were missing.

"Mayor Humdinger!" Ryder exclaimed. "He hates dogs. But where is he taking them?"

Liberty had an idea. She planned to get herself dognapped to lead the team to Chase.

Liberty's plan worked. Soon she was scooped up by Mayor Humdinger's goons. They took Liberty to the dog jail, where she spotted Chase.

Chase didn't think he deserved to be rescued. "I used to think I was a hero," Chase told her. "It turns out I'm just scared."

"Heroes get scared," Liberty told Chase gently. "But they push through and keep going. That's what makes them heroes."

Chase felt better, but he told Liberty that the doors were locked and there was no way out.

"I forgot to tell you," said Liberty. "I brought backup."

Just then, Rubble's wrecking ball made a big hole in the wall. The dogs were free!

Back at headquarters, the PAW Patrol saw storm clouds gathering over Humdinger Heights — a giant building that was Mayor Humdinger's latest addition to the city. Sensing trouble, the team got ready to head to the tower.

"Do you ever wonder what it would be like to be an official member of the team?" Ryder asked Liberty.

"Only, like, all the time!" Liberty said.

Ryder presented the little dog with a rocket-powered scooter. Liberty couldn't believe it — she was going to be part of the PAW Patrol!

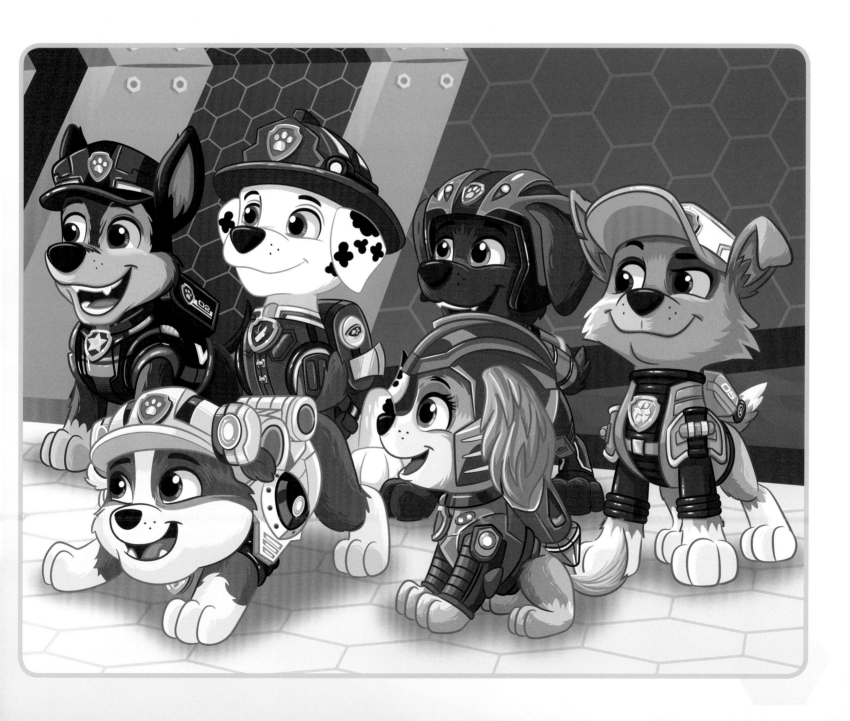

"Welcome to the team!" they cheered
when Liberty roared up to them.
There was no time to waste!

At Humdinger Heights, the wind had started to blow, and hail the size of basketballs fell from the sky. "Rocky, Marshall, get those people inside," said Ryder. "Zuma, Liberty, make sure the streets are clear."

Zuma saw a car with a family in it sinking in the canal! He dove into the water with his submarine, and Liberty hopped onto his rescue raft. She sped after Zuma, and soon he and the people from the car burst through the surface of the water and got onto the raft.

"Way to go!" Liberty cheered, steering Zuma and the family to safety.

Meanwhile, Ryder and Chase had rescued Mayor Humdinger, and Skye had stopped his weather machine, which was the cause of the chaos. The PAW Patrol had saved Adventure City again! Humdinger would no longer be mayor.

"You mess with our city, you're going to get what's coming to you," Liberty told the foolish mayor.

The next day, there was a big celebration at city hall. The PAW Patrol was given a key to the city for all their hard work.

"Pup, pup, hooray!" they cheered.

"Let's hear it for Marshall, Rubble, Chase, Rocky, Zuma, Skye — and the newest member of the PAW Patrol, Liberty!" said Ryder.

Liberty looked out at the cheering crowd, happy she could help save her city.

Hooray, Liberty!

THE END

Be part of the action in the PAW Patrol Movie Sticker Book!

Bursting with activities and plenty of stickers, this is the PAWfect book for fans of the PAW Patrol movie!

9780755502653